ALL TOO WOMAN

Dr. Shalaka Samant

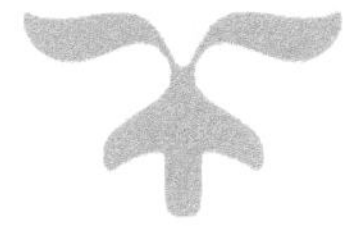

BOOKSQUIRREL PUBLICATION

BookSquirrel Publication

Mahadev Totala Nager, Indore (M.P), 452001
Regd Under MSME
Website: *www.booksquirrelpublication.com*

"All Too Woman"

By: Dr. Shalaka Samant

ISBN: *978-81-949648-7-2*

English Fictional Novel 1st Edition

Book Formatting: Mr_Ash

Cover Design: Ronak Chavda

Illustrations: Sudakshina

Acknowledgements and Dedication

I dedicate this book to my parents, Nisha and Sharad. I owe them for all that I am today and will be tomorrow.

I would like to thank Sudakshina for her thoughtful and pertinent artwork for which I had no inputs to provide as I completely lack the ability to create anything artistic.

I would like to thank my sister, Dr. Shantala Samant, for her criticism and feedback about the stories presented here.

I would also like to thank my husband, Kedar and daughter, Swara for their support in helping me write these stories.

Dr. Shalaka Samant

MISUNDERSTOOD

A sea of numbers and graphs floated in front of her on the computer screen, but she could make no sense of any of it. The large cuckoo clock on her office cabin wall – the only obnoxiously expensive; impulse buy that Sheela had made in her life- ticked away, rather noisily, reminding her that it was evening already and everyone had left for home. A storm of thoughts waged inside her head. There was a deadline to prepare a convincing presentation to showcase her company's achievements in the last financial year to the stakeholders and clinch an important deal. The responsibility to give it her best shot, over the weekend, rested squarely on her shoulders. Sheela was the chief financial analyst for her firm. She had trained at the Yale Business School following a stellar academic career in some of the best business schools in India. Upon her return to India, she had been a coveted employee and many firms vied for her attention, but she had settled for Agrinext, a non-profit organization which promoted innovation in agriculture. Sheela had always been the quintessential philanthropist from an early age, ensuring she passed on her pencil boxes, books, and toys to needy children. The altruistic business model of Agrinext, therefore, strongly beckoned to her, though she could have demanded a heftier salary at any other multinational company. This presentation that she was struggling to prepare would have been a piece of cake on any other day, but today was different.

Sheela sat at her desk focusing hard on the numbers. There had always been minor distractions on other days. She would often forget to water the few plants she had in her balcony at home. Then she would have to call home and request her mother-in-law to do it for her. Her thoughts floated to her mother-in-law – a strong lady herself; a retired teacher. Sheela felt a moment of solace in remembering her mother-in-law as she knew that she was the one person who would be by her side in what was to come. Queerly enough, she suddenly thought of the saas-bahu[1] sitcoms on TV and how the relationships between these women were always shown in a bad light. She uttered a silent prayer that her life was so different. Suddenly, she remembered she needed to pay the electricity bill, the phone bill, and the maid. 'Had she done the laundry in the morning?' – Sheela dismissed these mundane worries and tried to look at the graphs again. 'Had she read it right?' – a thought flashed. Her thoughts jumped again and rested on her parents. What was she supposed to tell them? 'Maybe a cup of coffee will help to soothe my nerves? Or would it fray them even more? Plus, I hate the runny, old coffee from the machine' – she thought to herself. Sheela got up, determined to do something about this funny state of her mind, grabbed her coffee mug, and moved to the cabin door. Then she muttered something to herself, replaced the mug, picked up her computer, packed her bag and rushed to her car to drive back home. Sheela thought, once home she would order a hot chicken biryani and collect her scattered thoughts. Today was a Friday and no one would be home in the evening. Her mother-in-law was visiting her sister and it was bowling night for Sheela's husband.

She reached home to be greeted with a big meow and several attention-seeking brushes against her leg from Jeremy, her pet cat. Sheela had found Jeremy on her stroll in New Haven; abandoned on a cold, winter night in a dark alley. A meekly purring kitten then,

[1]"Saas-bahu" which literally means "Mother-in-law - daughter-in-law" is a popular style of soap operas on Indian television depicting the frequent feuds between these two.

Jeremy had brushed against her leg the same way he did today. She had taken him in and he had been her close confidante ever since. She strongly considered rattling out her feelings to him before she did to anyone else and calm herself, but then she realized she was famished. She hurriedly picked up her phone and browsed her favorite food ordering app. First, she ordered a biryani alone, but then at checkout as the app prompted her to order some (much needed) alcohol too, Sheela succumbed to the desire. Although there was a tangled mess of apprehension, suspicion, anger, and jealousy in her head, she set about tidying up the house till the food arrived. Sheela could afford a maid and more with the combined salaries of herself and her husband. But she categorically maintained that keeping her home clean and tidy could best be achieved by her alone. She picked up a broom and mop and cleaned till the doorbell rang signalling the arrival of the food delivery man. As she opened the door the hot summer, night air blew in and she was reminded that she needed to sit down and deal with the confusion in her mind that had been momentarily swept away with the frantic cleaning she had undertaken. She carefully laid out her food on the table near the sofa and sat down. Jeremy sat next to her, gently purring, hoping for some chicken to come his way. Sheela recollected what had disturbed her so much last night.

Sheela had returned home late last night from work to find her husband and mother-in-law already asleep. She had quietly eaten at the dinner table and decided to wind down for the day when she saw it. Her husband had the habit of writing a personal diary and she had never read anything in it. She prided herself on the fact that she and her husband shared an open and honest relationship with nothing to hide from one another. She had never checked his emails, phone, or even his diary. That night, she saw his diary was lying on the dinner table and curiosity nudged her to open it. Most entries were routine – in some he had poured his heart out about the stress at work and in others he had entered food or workout logs. But the entries from last week stood out. Every page showed "I MISS HER" scribbled over and over again. Sheela's mind raced. *'Who did he miss?'* She knew he had recently bumped into his college girlfriend at an office party. He had shared his past with Sheela and she knew they had dated for about two years before parting ways as the woman had decided to move to another city for work. *'It must be her'* – she had thought.

Sheela continued to mull over these thoughts with her biryani. Sheela walked to the mirror in the room and looked at herself. Although she had never met this other woman, she imagined her to be very beautiful which 'justified' her husband missing her. Sheela, on the other hand, had not exercised for a month now and she could see a tiny paunch showing from under her dress. Her hair was thin and lifeless. She did not remember the last time she had visited a salon. As she dwelled upon these thoughts, Sheela was not aware of the number of glasses of the fancy wine she had consumed. She had not eaten any food at all. She got up to put the, now cold, biryani in the fridge. As soon as she turned, Jeremy got in her way. She stumbled, fell over a stool, in her inebriated state, and came crashing to the floor, face down.

She opened her bleary eyes when the cat, all seven pounds of squirming flesh, climbed onto her belly. Squinting into the sunlight streaming in from the open window, she discovered that she was now the weary possessor of a pounding headache, and at some point, had managed to lose both a tooth and a spouse. The events from last night leading to her fall were now a blur but she remembered thinking of her husband's crush. She had certainly lost him to this new, beautiful lady. The pain from her missing tooth was nothing to bear in comparison. She tried to push herself up and noticed there was a soft mattress beneath her and not the hard floor that she had fallen on. She was in her bed. 'What had happened after her fall?

How had she come to her bed?' Her headache was making it difficult for her to remember the happenings of the night before. Someone walked over and kissed her softly on the forehead. It was her husband. She wanted to shout for joy and hug him as tight as she could but she was unable to get up quickly. All she managed was a short, confused giggle. As he sat beside her with her hand in his, she mustered all her strength and asked the one question that had been plaguing her for the longest time now, 'Who do you miss?'. She could not tell if the expression on her husband's face changed, as her headache continued to nag her, but she thought she saw a smile. He moved close to her and said, "You! Who else did you think, dumbo?" Although her physical pain had not lessened, her mental anguish vanished. She knew her husband never lied to her. When he said that he missed her then that was the truth and there was no one else. All her confused thoughts fell in place. Without him having to explain, she realized how her passion for her work meant long working hours and being away from home meant she barely spent any time with her husband. She remembered the Sunday mornings when they would jog together, attack cryptic crossword clues over a leisurely brunch, and watch movies huddled up with each other at night. All of those seemed like things of the past. She was so focused on her work that she had forgotten the one person who loved and respected her for the woman she was. She realized her folly and how she had misinterpreted the diary notes. With a strong resolve to undo the misunderstanding she said, "I am famished. Let's warm up the biryani from last night and eat it while we watch a scary movie." He nodded in agreement and she knew she could make all well again.

Dr. Shalaka Samant

REFLECTED

Sania stepped onto the train to get to work. It was in the wee hours of the morning, but Houston was not a city to require a sweater in the fall. She donned the only pair of denims she owned with a t-shirt that had the peeling remnants of her graduate school logo printed on it. Sania was habituated to starting her day very early and she would be the first person to unlock her lab doors. She had been working in the field of drug discovery for meningitis as a postdoctoral fellow at Rice University for two years now and had diligently continued this practice, of going to work early from her graduate student days. In fact, everything Sania did was timely, meticulous, and carefully planned. She would work in her lab until 5:30 pm every day, take the train back home, throw in a Kathy Smith workout video into the CD player, workout for half an hour, cook a simple Indian meal, watch some television and go to bed sharp at 9 pm. It was a Friday today, and that meant she would do her weekly groceries at the local store. Tomorrow she would call home, as was her routine, to talk to her parents in Mumbai over the weekend.

As she mulled over the experiments she had lined up for today, she noticed that the train was particularly crowded. She was used to an empty train this early during the day, and she would always manage to get into the same compartment and get the same window seat below an advertisement with a friendly gecko urging readers to buy their auto insurance. Today, she had to jostle her way through several football fans, carrying all their paraphernalia and arguing enthusiastically about the outcome of the game, to even board the train. That is when she remembered that today was an important football game. As she inched ahead, she held on to her bag tightly, afraid of pickpockets – a gesture that is inbuilt in the DNA of anyone from Mumbai. Sania was not even sure if she should expect a pickpocket here. Only once had such a person succeeded in conning her while in Mumbai. However, to the poor pickpocket's consternation, all that he could get out of Sania's bag was a bunch of flashcards meant for revising her vocabulary as she prepared for her GRE test. She had stashed these cards into a purse and 'flaunted' it in the outermost pocket of her bag. It was a 'fat purse' with several flashcards – loads of words but no money. Sania smiled as she imagined the thief's expression upon opening the purse.

She was finally successful in inching towards her favorite spot near the gecko board, but as she raised herself up on her toes to catch a glimpse of her usual seat, she noticed her seat had been taken by an old lady who was talking animatedly in Spanish to her neighbour. Sania was reminded of her teenage years in Mumbai. Making her way through a crowded train, with fellow passengers shouting at her for carrying a huge bag, only to find most seats taken, used to be a part of her daily routine. The only difference, she thought, between her train ride today and the one in Mumbai, was that on days when she was particularly tired to keep standing throughout the hour-long journey, she could request the three people sitting on a three-seater train seat to "adjust" and make some room for a fourth, weary passenger to rest. These requests often resulted in the seated passengers merely pretending to move, and the onus then resting entirely on the traveller requesting the extra seat, to use her skill, and accommodate herself in the almost invisible space created. On rare occasions, just enough space would be made for the fourth passenger and she could rest her tired self adequately. Sania carefully moved ahead, and despite today's rush, found a quiet corner to retire. She now stood facing the sun. Sania loved the sun. At this particular time of the day it shone on her just enough to make her feel warm. As she pulled out a book from her bag, someone tapped eagerly on her shoulder. Sania turned around to notice an African-American girl, with soft, brown curls lining her face, big black eyes covered with broad-rimmed glasses, and a bold dash of purple lipstick across her lips asking her, 'Would you happen to have a mirror on you?'

Sania looked at her bag. It was an old, black satchel, with the details of the conference, where it had been handed out as a freebie, painted on it in large letters. Its only contents, Sania knew, were her book, a scarf to cover her hair, her purse, her keys, her lunch-box and her cell-phone. Other inhabitants like research articles, a sweater, mittens and an umbrella kept getting added and removed based on their need. Sania had never owned a pocket mirror to carry in her bag; neither did she carry any cosmetics with her. This sudden question about the existence of a mirror in her bag – probably a quintessential occupant of the purses of other women – and her inability to produce one, made her aware, of how she felt different from other women. Sania quickly recovered from this request, pretended to actually have a mirror on her, and after rapidly scrummaging through her bag for the non-existent beauty essential, made her best attempt at signalling a "forgot-to-pack-it-today-but-I-normally-have-it" no. On the rest of the short train ride, no matter how much she tried to focus on her book, she could not take her mind off her inability to produce as tiny a thing as a mirror from her bag. In her mind, the mirror symbolized inadequacy.

Sania had always found herself inadequate – inadequate in her ability to stand up to the typical definitions of beauty laid out by people around her. Her first encounter with beauty and *her* lack of it came about when she was a very young child, through her conversations with her paternal grandmother – her primary caregiver in the absence of her working parents. Sania's grandmother hailed from a remote village in Maharashtra, and her definition of beauty, as is true for most Indians, rested solely on the presence of light skin. Her grandmother proclaimed, rather unapologetically, that fair-skinned people are beautiful, and went on to tell Sania that her fair-skinned cousins were more beautiful than her. Courtesy of this early opinionated conditioning, Sania too began believing that fair-skinned people were beautiful. Her dark skin made her feel inadequate. When she started school, she met more such people who brazenly bullied her for her dark complexion. Sania was too young to understand that they did it to cover their own ineptness at learning. As if the lack of fair skin was not enough, she also had an overbite - her upper teeth protruded over her lower jaw. This led to her being jeered at even more. Sania was deeply pained when she remembered how, her boyfriend of several years, had also quickly pointed out, once their relationship got a little serious, that they should do something about her "buck teeth". She was a smart, independent, and hard-working individual but these physical inadequacies, as she had been made to believe, took a significant toll on her confidence. She steered clear of student gatherings, holiday parties, and other social events. Any place that even remotely carried the reputation of having a sizeable number of people, at any given time, was strictly avoided by Sania. She found peace in her secluded lab even on weekends. During lunch hour, she would finish her lunch quickly and get back to her bench before any other lab members would go out for lunch. Just as she was shy and scared of people, she also hated mirrors. She barely managed to catch a glimpse of herself in the mirror, before she left for work, to avoid looking bedraggled. The woman on the train, asking her for a mirror, made all these memories resurface and Sania felt shaken. When the train came to a stop at her station, Sania's mind was so clouded with thoughts that she almost forgot to get off. The strong scent of fried dough wafting towards her from a doughnut cart that sold its wares near her station jerked Sania out of her reverie, reminding her that it was her turn to get off, and she stepped out into the sunny morning.

She walked towards the medical school building. As was customary, Sania climbed two flights of stairs, reached her lab, and unlocked the door since she was the first occupant of the premises. After placing her things at her desk, she went to the bathroom. She completed her business, all the while hoping that she should not meet someone she knew, otherwise she would be forced to exchange social niceties. As she came out of the stall and started washing her hands, she saw her adversary, a huge mirror, staring back at her. She quickly turned away but before she did, she noticed she was not alone. The mirror reflected someone else. She saw Jill, crouched underneath one of the sinks lining the opposite wall, sobbing inconsolably.

Jill was the most beautiful girl in the Department of Neurosciences, where Sania worked. She had an undergraduate degree from Harvard and a doctoral degree from an acclaimed lab at University of Houston. She was tall with bright blue eyes, long, wavy, blond hair and most important of all, she had the unmistakable mark of a beautiful person, according to Sania – fair skin. Sania had never dared to talk to Jill as she was fearful such a beautiful person might not acknowledge her presence. She was startled today to see this beautiful, confident, girl cowering and crushed. Sania's first instinct was to act invisible, keep looking at her toes, and walk out as she would usually do. This time she was not just terribly shy but also not sure of what to do when someone was so dejected. Something made her stop on her way out and she turned back and slowly made her way towards Jill. Sensing approaching footsteps, Jill looked up and Sania saw that she was nothing like the pretty and confident Jill she knew. The crying had led to black streaks of eye make-up across her face and her foundation was washed away in places, making her face look like a landscape marked by a network of rivers. Sania was dumbfounded when Jill threw herself at Sania with a loud 'Sania!' A cry pierced through Sania's mind 'How could Jill know my name? That is unbelievable.' Sania was always confused about the best way to hug people, even in regular interactions, and often ended up groping their behinds. Here Jill was falling all over her in her grief and Sania had no clue how to react. She did not have to do much as Jill started pouring her heart out. 'It is Sam. He dumped me and you know why, just because he thinks I have flat feet. After all these years together, *that was his excuse*!' Jill sobbed uncontrollably as Sania awkwardly held her arms around her, making sure she hovered around the back and did not go lower for fear of being inappropriate. She, the ugly, dark Sania – as she had been made to believe by people around her – was consoling the fair and gorgeous Jill. The only words that came to Sania's mind as she patted Jill's back in an ungainly manner were, 'Why are you crying? You are so beautiful!' She thought to herself, 'Fair people have it all. Or do they?' Sania looked at the mirror on the wall across, this time more confidently than she had before, and *reflected* once again on the definition of beauty and the fairness of it all.

UNFETTERED

The elevator came to a stop and the doors opened to let her in. The elevator, though large enough to accommodate eight people as well as the apparently five hundred and sixty kilograms of resulting weight, always made her feel claustrophobic. Of the two in her building, Sofia would categorically avoid the elevator without glass panels at the back, no matter how late she was for work. The elevator with glass panels let light in and she could see the bustling commercial district below. Although she was still confined to a closed space while riding this elevator, the perceived proximity to living beings and fresh air outside mildly assuaged her phobia. Sofia pushed the button to reach the thirteenth floor where her office was. She convinced herself that working on the thirteenth floor was not a bad omen. After all, the ground floor of the building was labelled as the first floor which meant that her office was technically the twelfth floor. It had been ten years since she had been working at this prestigious law firm in Mumbai. Strangely enough, the inauspicious nature of the establishment, with respect to the floor on which it was located, had never bothered her. The last few months had been different.

Something was bothering her today but she could not pinpoint what it was. She reminisced about the time when the elevator had shuddered to a stop during a power outage. All the lights went out. It was pitch dark and hot inside. In a hurry to get home and meet her friend, she had forgotten to take the glass elevator. Fortunately, she had started looking at her cell-phone to keep her company but her feet had begun to shake and her heart was racing. This continued for a couple of minutes and Sofia started sweating profusely. She felt unseen chains fettering her to where she stood and she could not move. She was so frantic that she used all her strength and started clawing at the heavy, locked metal door in an attempt to pry it open.

The metal door opened momentarily, of its own accord, but she could not help secretly marvel at her strength which made her smile even in this adverse situation. Her smile soon faded as the door shut itself again, and her ordeal with being stuck in the powerless elevator, with no light or fresh air lasted another two minutes. Sofia was almost about to faint from her palpitations when the power was restored and the door opened completely. She remembered not using the elevator for a whole week after that.

The elevator moved swiftly to the fifth floor and stopped to let someone in. Not being the sole occupant of the elevator made Sofia a little less tense. But as a thin, bespectacled lady, in her fifties, walked in – her pencil heel shoes tapping hard at the floor – so marched in Sofia's awkward social skills. Sofia moved to the corner of the elevator as if she were all the remaining six people that could safely occupy the space. She was just short of crouching in the corner and the handrail dug into her back. The new occupant of the elevator had doused herself in so much perfume that Sofia felt a little dizzy. She wondered why people used so much perfume. *'Perhaps, they were trying to cover something more than just regular human body odour?'* The lady merely kept checking her watch and seemed to be running late for some chore. An elderly man boarded the elevator on the tenth floor and the *perfumed* lady uttered a flustered "Tsk". Sofia thought to herself that if this was such an important chore that she could not afford to lose the few seconds that the elevator stopped at its scheduled stops, this lady should have started a few minutes in advance. Finally, the old man and the lady disembarked at the twelfth floor and again Sofia was left alone, wishing for some respite from the heavily scented enclosure. In the few seconds that the elevator rose to her floor, Sofia could not help mull over how the elevator was a melting pot of such a wide variety of people and their temperaments, much like all the other places in

Mumbai where she had been living for the past ten years. People got in and got out of countless elevators across the city – many more around the world – with innumerable dreams, aspirations, grudges, joys, and stories. Some smiled or waved at others, some just moved about to allow more folks to squeeze their way in, most were engrossed in their cell-phones, while a few, like herself, tapped their feet nervously and waited for their destination to arrive.

Sofia arrived at her floor and her thoughts bounced back to her feeling of uneasiness. The top management at her workplace had changed and there were many changes being made in the roles and responsibilities of most employees. She had also noticed a change in her manager's attitude towards her. He had been a great mentor when she had started at this law firm, after completing her masters. The interview with him had made her realize instantly that *this* was where she wanted to work. Her mind raced to the first day at work, when he had put her at such ease, that she had almost ended up complaining about the discriminating questions posed by the company's human resource team. They had asked her about her marital status and upon hearing that she was single they had asked her about her plans to get married. Sofia had been shocked. She had trained at some of the best law schools across the world and such biased questions had never been a part of the interview. Her manager had discussed the situation with her in detail and had somehow managed to allay her apprehensions about the working conditions at the firm. From that day on, it had been a strong working relationship with numerous successes. They had worked together and won several law suits involving cola giants and instant noodle manufacturers. The triumphs had, of course, been dampened by some failures, but they both had managed to discuss these and strategize about the changes to be made to avoid such failures in the future. Things were very different now. Her manager had mentioned in a common meeting, that he felt, that while men were from Mars and women were from Venus, Sofia was from Jupiter. She knew he was hinting at her social ineptness but was perplexed by his public reference to the same. Sofia was a very able lawyer and she strongly believed that given her track record over the long association with the firm she would soon be made partner. But there were no tell-tale signs of this happening which puzzled her further.

Sofia was a quiet individual outside of work. She had been quiet and soft-spoken as a child. She only managed to bag the *dumb* parts of trees, animals, or goddesses in school plays. If she did manage to get a part with a dialogue, it was the part of a boy. Any parts with a dialogue would see her playing a boy. She would often have to sport a moustache or beard and wear a *lungi* while her friends serenaded in pretty dresses. Nothing dampened Sofia's spirit though. Her work was her passion. She was a polar opposite of her social self in a meeting or courtroom proceeding. Here she unleashed a booming voice and compelling arguments that would make anyone stop in their tracks and pay attention. But her ability to bond with people, and be part of the regular office gossip and politics, was poor. Most people who saw her at work felt intimidated by her prowess and would never befriend her. She thought she had found a good friend at work in her manager, but now she felt alienated. As she walked towards her desk she was once again reminded of the stark disparity in standards at her office. A male colleague who had joined only a year ago and had little to his credit since, had been given a personal cabin to work in while Sofia, a long-time, outstanding employee continued to work as part of the open office space. This particular colleague had befriended practically the entire office in his short stint and would be seen more at the water fountain – chatting people up for gossip – than at his desk. It appeared as if gossip was his life-blood and Sofia squirmed in her chair at his loathsome behaviour.

The experience of interacting with many such gossip-mongering sycophants, every day at work, was even more stifling for Sofia than being stuck alone in the elevator. She wondered what made such people succeed. They lacked calibre and made no attempts at working hard; yet they were able to climb the corporate ladder. '*Did they have some magic up their sleeves? Or was it that the corporate world, for some mysterious reason, favoured the obsequious chatterboxes with no apparent laurels?*' She convinced herself she could never arrive at the right answer, if there was one.

Sofia started her work for the day. She was supposed to brief her manager about a new law suit involving a famous businessman. It was a delicate affair and the firm needed the best heads to come together to build the case. Sofia had worked late last night and identified some key points that could shed light on the mysteries that surrounded the case. She wanted to urgently discuss these with her manager. She walked briskly to her manager's cabin – *he had a cabin; he was a guy after all* – and after a polite knock let herself in. He had a smug smile on his face. He did not offer her a seat, but she took one anyways because she knew this would be a long discussion. Before she could start, he said, 'We need to go in different directions.' Sofia thought she was being taken off this case and assigned another one given all the upheavals that were happening at her firm. Her manager continued, 'Today will be your last day here. Your dues for this month and the appropriate severance pay as per the company policy will be paid to you shortly.' Sofia was completely dumbfounded. She did not feel anger, just a bitter sense of being cheated. She had devoted a long time to building this firm and its reputation and now she was being told to leave immediately without any explanation. The feeling of betrayal was so strong, that despite several years of training and practice in law, she did not care to ask for an explanation for this sudden action. She quietly gathered her papers and walked towards her desk not bothering to look back. She deleted all the files she had created for her new case from her desktop as she held back the tears welling up in her eyes. Sofia knew this supposed act of retribution was worthless as the IT guys could retrieve the lost files, but she did it nonetheless.

She gathered her belongings. She did not have many on her desk. Sofia hated flaunting her personal life at work, unlike the others who kept a myriad collection of things like pictures of family, postcards and souvenirs from trips, and their kids' drawings. Sofia wondered what she would do next, but she was too numbed by the recent turn of events to think clearly. As she got into the glass elevator to go home, she saw through the transparent elevator walls, beneath her the streets teeming with people going about their jobs. The fact that she did not have one gnawed at her. She almost felt like she had committed a crime by being declared redundant. She wondered what she would say to her friends who still had jobs. Suddenly, there was a power outage and the elevator stopped. This time however, her usual fear of closed, dark places did not creep in. She stood alone in the dark chamber absorbing the news and contemplating about what to do next. In the face of her hectic and high-strung work life unexpectedly jarring to a halt, the stalled elevator did not irk her at all. Several minutes passed by but there was no sign of the elevator coming back to life. Surprisingly, Sofia did not panic. She just remembered all her successes at work and felt good. The loss of her job, which had been her identity all these years, was overwhelming and stifling but she was confident she would find something new to excel at. Sofia had always found a new purpose whenever life had knocked her out and she knew she would this time too. The power was restored and the elevator slowly reached the ground floor and the doors opened onto the street. No longer chained by her fear of small places and inhibited by the monstrous loss she had just suffered, Sofia looked at the busy, scuttling, employed people everywhere on the street and smiled before stepping out to join them.

ENCIRCLED

She was making rotis. The heat from the small earthen stove drifted towards her in waves. She felt parched but did not move to fetch some water for herself. Sumitra knew that if she let the fire die, she would have to blow through the small metal pipe to reignite the flames. This would mean unwanted anguish caused by the coughing and breathlessness it would induce. The task at hand, of making the last two pieces of bread, had to be completed promptly. She rolled out the dough while wiping the sweat off her brow with the back of her palm. Sumitra was making the rotis for her family. Family; she smirked, as she thought of how this word was a mere verbal representation of the group formed by herself, her father and her elder brother. She was home today on a week-long break from her work in the city and had been assigned the same chore she wished she would never have to do again when she left home for a new beginning in the city.

Sumitra had never known her mother. In the remote village in Gujarat, where she was born, there was no hospital even today. Only recently had a retired army doctor had set up a small clinic. As a child, she remembered only being treated with home remedies. A rather stubborn fever would require the services of the local witch doctor. Following the abstruse rituals, the ailing family waited, while the miraculous machine that the human body is, mended itself; further reconfirming the naïve beliefs of the villagers in the healing powers of witchcraft. Many infants and mothers died during delivery and the same had been the fate of Sumitra's mother. Sumitra knew she was lucky to have survived. She always told herself that her mother had shielded her from death and embraced it in place of Sumitra. She loved staring at the only tattered photo she carried of her mother in her purse. Sumitra's mother had long, shiny jet-black hair tied back into a perfectly coiled bun. There was a tattoo in between her eyebrows resembling the mathematical operator for division. The long hours of toil in the tiny barren field – that grudgingly allowed the family a harvest of wheat, barely enough to feed everyone – showed on her face. Although she was only a young twenty-two-year-old when the photo was taken, just before Sumitra was born, she had leathery skin, baked into place by the torturous sun she had to face each day at work. The only piece of jewellery she owned was a pair of golden peacock eardrops; delicate golden wires made the feathery plume with fanned tips adorning their crests. The shiny peacocks, the sole 'prosperous' trinket adorning Sumitra's mother's visage stood out in stark contrast to her patched sari and torn slippers. There was a hint of a weary yet confident smile on her face as her hand was lightly placed on her rounded belly. It appeared as if she were reassuring her unborn child that she was there for her. Each time Sumitra stared at the photo she longed to hug her mother- her only *real* family she achingly missed.

Sumitra's father had never acknowledged her presence in the household. After her mother had passed away, he had called upon a distant, widowed relative to run the household for a few years until Sumitra became old enough to cook and clean. Then she had been relegated to the position of a homemaker for her father. He had never appreciated her nor chided her, never hugged her or hit her. Her little hands had cooked the rotis, washed the clothes and vessels, mopped the floor and helped out in the field. How she wished her mother were there to wipe the sweat off her brow, make her food or just pat her to sleep on her lap. The only good thing that her father had done for her was to put her in school. It had probably, merely been a convenient gesture to let her tag along with her elder brother as they both trudged the couple of kilometres that separated Sumitra's home from her school. The walk to school was long but definitely less laborious than the walk to draw water from an ancient well, several kilometres away. At home, her brother occupied centre-stage. He was the first to eat dinner and had clean clothes for school every day. It did not matter to Sumitra's father that all her brother did at school – if he reached school on time, as his time was best spent in climbing trees, throwing stones at stray animals, and dreaming endlessly – was to call upon himself the wrath of the school master. To her utter embarrassment, Sumitra's brother was often spotted standing outside his class sporting an impish and arrogant smile. Unlike her 'family', Sumitra's school world had been a source of love and joy for her. It was here she was surrounded by her loving teachers and friends. The pain in her heart, of being an abandoned child, despite having a home and a family to go back to everyday, was greatly assuaged by the lessons that had piqued her curiosity. Playtime with her friends had been the most treasured part of Sumitra's day.

Then one day, her world had come crashing down as she had overheard her father talking to a neighbour mentioning that he could not afford school education for Sumitra anymore and was only keen on continuing his son's education. He had even mentioned getting Sumitra married in a couple of years. She was only ten and this conversation had left her completely heartbroken. Help had come her way soon though. The social worker who used to visit Sumitra's school every month had told little Sumitra one day that a kind lady, who lived in a far-off city Ahmedabad, had agreed to pay all the money needed to support her education till she graduated. Sumitra had not understood much except that someone was willing to help her go to school every day. She had been overjoyed. Later, the social worker had visited her home with the village head and they both had coerced her father into letting her go to school. Sumitra was a diligent learner and had soon completed her school and college education supported by the monetary help from the good samaritan who had stepped in at the right time. Her academic success had helped her secure a job and she had got a chance to move away from the drudgery of being with her father and brother.

The smell of burning dough wafted to her nose and pulled Sumitra back to the present. She had forgotten a perfectly round roti for too long over the open flame. She quickly removed the burnt piece, reproaching herself for dreaming away when she was late to serve dinner to her father and brother. She had decided to visit her family during this break, imagining she would tell them stories from the city, and bring them gifts, and almost magically make the missing warmth return. She wanted to re-establish the bond of family. That was a possibility in her mind as she was no longer the inconsequential girl child meant to cook and clean, but was an independent and educated woman. She felt she had returned to the family dynamic on a higher footing than before and could make amends. Instead of the happy reunion she had pictured in her mind though, Sumitra had received a cold welcome. Only an uncle who lived in her village, and who was proud of all she had single-handedly achieved, had come to receive her at the train station and now here she was cooking a meal for herself and the two 'strangers' who hungrily paced the short distance of the room outside. She felt like the hapless lioness who has the power and intelligence to kill strong and agile prey but submits to the instinct of surrendering the kill, only to maintain order in the pride, to the male lion who prowls impatiently. After a quiet meal, where nobody appreciated the effort behind putting food on the table, Sumitra lay awake and thought of how she was going to spend the rest of her break with her disinterested and unloving family.

Seeing no purpose in trying to bond with her family anymore, she decided to meet her benefactor instead. Sumitra thought that would be a more fulfilling use of her time away from work – letting her mentor know she had managed to do well for herself courtesy of her selfless donations. Early the next day Sumitra travelled to Ahmedabad. She had enquired about where the kind lady lived and was determined to meet her. She wanted to fall at her feet; maybe even hug her, as Sumitra strongly believed this was the second boon her mother had sent her way. When she reached Ahmedabad towards noon, the city was abuzz with activity. People were hurrying to their various destinations, sellers were selling their wares on the road and in shops, children were returning from school and cattle sat munching on their fodder, swatting flies with their dung-crusted tails. Sumitra felt hungry and decided to get a samosa from a small shop she spotted a few feet away from her bus stop. The pleasant shopkeeper promptly held out two piping hot samosas. As she deliberately chewed on her food contemplating how her meeting with her benefactor would go, she noticed a gaunt and emaciated boy, almost her age, walk in cautiously. He hungrily eyed all the hot snacks on display in the shop. His back was slightly hunched and he carried a black bag falling apart at the seams, probably containing his work things. He warily reached into his shirt pocket, and holding out the lone ten rupee note he found there, started pleading with the shopkeeper to give him lunch. The shopkeeper's demeanour was completely different from when he had pleasantly interacted with Sumitra. He was bothered by this unwanted customer at a time when other profitable customers were flocking in and he barked at the boy, 'All you can get for that much is a single samosa'. Sumitra could see tears welling up in the boy's eyes – eyes that were so weary it was an effort to even tear up. With a defeated look on his face, that made his shoulders droop even more, the boy accepted the lone samosa. Sumitra felt her stomach wrench. She almost got up to offer her food to this boy but quickly stopped herself. She was alone in a new city. She thought, 'Should

I offer him money instead?' but dropped that idea too as it appeared no better than offering a stranger food. She finished her food, looking at the hungry boy eating the samosa that barely satiated him. A sudden pang of guilt tugged at her heart. She felt deeply ashamed of herself for being able to afford all the food she wanted and cursed herself for not acting upon the impulse to share what she had.

She got up to walk towards her benefactor's home as it was close by and this would allow her to explore the city more. Soon she spotted a cycle rickshaw which made her change her mind as she had never travelled in one. She eagerly hailed the rickshawala. When he stopped near her, she could see him clearly. Long trips in the harsh sun, pushing hard at the never-serviced rickshaw had made his skin coarse and wrinkled. She guessed he was probably in his late fifties but the wrinkles on his skin were hardened like it had never seen any collagen before. He had long bony arms with battered nails probably from doing other laborious tasks to make ends meet. In front of her stood an older version of the hungry boy in the snack shop that Sumitra had just exited. She asked him how much would he charge for her trip. Through what was left of his falling teeth came a meek, 'Fifteen rupees madam.' Sumitra, who had by now taken several cab rides in the city where she worked, was astonished at the low price he had quoted. As she raised her hand to beckon him to come along, the rickshawala – who was accustomed to customers haggling over even such a minimal fee – immediately clarified, 'Not one rupee less madam'. This quick protective response made Sumitra's heart cry. She was not going to argue over the fare anyways. In fact, she was ready to pay another fifteen. She quietly boarded the rickshaw and sat watching as the stalls, shops, buildings, people, and animals of the city rolled past her while the rickshawala pedalled with all his might. Sumitra wanted to enquire about his health, get to know if there was anyone to care for him at home – if he had a home that is.

She wanted to know if he had children; if he did, were they going to school. She was reminded of her kind benefactor again and how her help had made her an independent woman today despite the hardships at home. Again, she felt the hands of guilt encircling her thoughts; she was blessed to have found a mentor but what about this rickshawala's kids. 'Did they even have enough food and a shelter?', she thought. Her train of thoughts was interrupted as they reached her destination. While getting down Sumitra contemplated handing out a fifty rupee note to the rickshawala but then thought to herself what would he think. 'Would he think she was showing off her affluence? Would he start searching for change to take only the fifteen rupees he 'deserved'? Would she seem too vain saying "Keep the change." Too many thoughts crowded together in her mind. All she could do was count out the exact change and look away as the weary old man resumed his search for more passengers.

No sooner had she turned around; Sumitra's eyes caught another agonising sight. A beggar-woman was breast-feeding her infant, squatting next to a dilapidated wall on the road. It was noon and the sun shone bright on her and her baby's head. They had no fancy hats to cover their bare heads as they baked in the sun. Sumitra could spot every single bone in the woman's body and wondered when her last meal had been. Her lips were parched and her skin caked with dirt from not having bathed for days. Sumitra wondered whether she made any milk at all that the baby was feeding on. It was no wonder then that the baby looked equally malnourished; it had a big round belly and pencil thin limbs. Sumitra felt a strong tug at her heart looking at the child and mother clinging to each other; the mother attempting to partly save themselves from the sun and from the lecherous oglers –who could not even let such a pure connection be – and to partly pass on love and whatever feed she could make. This time neither the fear of a new city nor the apprehension of the consequences of helping a complete stranger shackled her. Even before she knew it, she reached out with her scarf that was large enough to cover them both from the prying eyes of the passers-by. The woman held up her hand to bless Sumitra. Again, a storm of questions, too many 'what-ifs' and 'buts' started slowing her down, but she brushed them aside by asking herself 'Would she be here today without her benefactor reaching out to help a little girl in a remote village she had never heard of? Wouldn't she still be rolling out circles of dough next to a hot stove for an unloving family?'. Her steps quickened as her mind cleared. She approached a nearby fruit vendor and quickly bought fruits and fresh water for the woman. Breaking the barrier of desperation and despondency that had caged her happiness for a long time now, a smile broke out on the woman's face. As she shook the coarse, cracked palms of the smiling beggar-woman – that faint yet invigorating smile brimming with hope, touched a deep corner of Sumitra's heart. Her purpose dawned upon her. She wanted to help. She wanted to bring more such smiles to unknown faces. She made a mental note of her next steps as she walked towards her benefactor's home. The bond she missed had been established and the circle was complete.

Dr. Shalaka Samant

ERASED

She picked up yet another one of those delicate orange flowers and tried to pass the needle she was holding through its thin yellow stem, which was only slightly wider than the needle. This time the needle pierced her finger instead of the stem and she was jerked out of the monotony of garland-making that had kept her busy for almost half a day now. The flowers she was trying to weave together had no strong smell. They had a characteristic flower-like scent, but nothing that would make them stand out amongst the more prolific and preferred jasmines and roses that often adorned garlands – just like Sakhi. Sakhi had tended to a small business in her younger years, and although she toiled at her work untiringly, it had never really blossomed into a huge enterprise. She did not need the money – not then not now. Her husband had been a successful entrepreneur himself. 'Was he in the next room while she made her garland?', Sakhi wondered, unsure of whether she was alone at home. She had wanted to make a mark for herself selling the hand-woven saris she carefully curated from distant villages all across India. However, she never managed to make huge profits and grow profusely. Wiping away the little pearl of blood that had formed at the site of the injury, she looked up from her flower pile and saw that the sun had now climbed up fairly high into the clear sky reminding her it was probably close to noon. But she was not quite sure if she had made any lunch at all. She felt hungry and thirsty and did not remember when she had last consumed water. As her thoughts formed a confusing mix inside her she watched a tractor tilling a large expanse of land near her home. The plough moved through the earth; its broad teeth deliberately separating the fat clumps of soil and forming small mounds on either side of the tool. Sakhi saw a bunch of crows flying down to sit in front of the plough's teeth, but quickly flying out of harm's way when the plough inched closer. It seemed to Sakhi that the farmer was harvesting a crop of crows.

The dry soil being loosened by the plough reminded Sakhi of the dryness clawing at her throat. She would have to get up from making her garland to drink water. She felt reluctant to leave. Besides, her feet ached and she could not remember where she had left the ointment her doctor had prescribed for her aching joints. She tried to rack her brains for the doctor's name, what his clinic looked like, what had happened at the last visit but drew a complete blank for all the questions she asked herself. She remembered having visited a doctor for treating the bouts of arthritis she suffered from but was unable to recall any information about the visits. Sakhi was now seventy-five and very little of her old self remained with her. She had developed dementia and very few memories were housed in her shrivelling brain which was once sharp and astute.

Sakhi had been the only child with no one else to feel close to in her immediate family other than her parents. It had been a very fortunate childhood. Having grown up in a house of plenty, she had never experienced the pain of denial or deprivation. Probably, by virtue of this abundance, she never lied, never threw a tantrum, never screamed or subscribed to any other typical form of rebellion that most children did. When her friends narrated how they had been beaten black and blue for misbehaving she was at a loss to comprehend their agony as she had never suffered thus. It worked both ways – she was very well-behaved, consequently her parents never reprimanded her. Since she had never been reproached or rebuked, a close bond had formed between Sakhi and her parents. They were her best friends and their sudden demise in a car crash just before her graduation had left her extremely forlorn and miserable. That is when her husband had entered her life. She was completing a master's degree in London and he was in the same graduate school. They had met at a graduate student party for celebrating an Indian festival. He was an amazing singer, and just like the many other girls at that party, Sakhi was smitten by his voice and stage presence. She was an inherently shy girl and the recent demise of her parents had further dampened her spirits so she did nothing about her crush. However, as her roommates forced her to attend more social events to make her forget her loss, she started seeing him more. They got talking and given that he had a very charming personality she had fallen for him. He had never asked her to marry him. He was happy being himself. But, Sakhi was keen on marrying him as she felt he could be her close friend. She thought he would easily fill the huge hole that losing her parents had burnt into her heart. He never said he loved her but Sakhi never gave up in the tussle to win him over, unlike her other female counterparts. It was sheerly based on her perseverance that Sakhi had persuaded him to marry her.

Perseverance and patient hard work had always been Sakhi's strong points. Be it her school, college, graduate school, business or family – she had always laboured away at the task at hand. But now, no matter how hard she tried to hold them back, dig them from the farthest recesses of her brain, her memories were dwindling away. The harder she tried, the harder it was for her to gather details. They would somehow manage to slip out of her grasp. She could not remember now how she had 'wooed' her husband. She could not remember what her wedding dress was like. She could not remember where they had been for their honeymoon. As she forced her brain to reveal some answers, she found herself staring at the cobwebs growing in the high corners of her comfortable home. The busy spider was spewing out more threads to catch an unsuspecting fly and manage dinner. She came back to the present as the thought of food reminded her of her growing hunger. The same questions plagued her again, 'Had she made any food?' 'Where had her husband been all this while?' He had never bothered to enquire about her health, but she should at least have seen him scurrying about the house minding his own business.' Puzzled, but not enough to get up and look around, Sakhi continued the trip down memory lane; down the crumbling remains of a once strong path.

The first couple of years of marriage had been blissful. Sakhi had inherited handsomely and they had spent their time travelling and enjoying all the good things that life had to offer. Her husband had started a firm dealing in real estate and he was doing well too. That is when they found out they were pregnant. Sakhi had never interacted closely with infants and toddlers as she had never been the kind to walk over to a toddler at the park or at the grocery store and start pinching its cheeks and uttering gibberish to grab his attention. She was the kind to lock herself up in her room if any guests with young children visited their home. She did not know what to do with them. Even if children her own age were a part of the visiting group, she would shy away from them. But the possibility of caring for her own child had changed her outlook. She was thrilled. Her husband did not care. He was busy building his business, too busy to notice his wife's joy when she revealed she was about to have a baby. She made the first couple of visits to the doctor alone, but for her six-week visit to detect a heart rate and confirm the growth of the foetus, she put her tenacity to test and persuaded her husband to come along. She wanted them to share the joy of listening to the first sign of life they both had created. The memory of that day was etched in her mind. Nothing could erase it – Sakhi believed. They arrived at the radiologist's clinic and waited for their turn while Sakhi drank obnoxious amounts of water to get ready for the ultrasound. Sakhi usually drank very little water, and as she painstakingly gulped down the liquid that day, she was reminded of her college friends referring to her as a camel. 'Strange what associations our brain makes and stores' – interestingly, this memory was easy to call upon. She clearly recollected her thoughts from that day as she stood in her kitchen now, hands over her hips, still wondering whether she had already cooked her meal. Her mind went back in time again and she saw herself in the imaging room now. The radiologist had put the probe on her stomach and uttered a sharp cry, 'Oh my god!' Sakhi had panicked and asked her what was wrong. The radiologist had said that Sakhi had many fibroids, the size of apples, on her uterus. More importantly, she had been unable to detect a heartbeat although she could see a mass that resembled a foetus. Sakhi's heart had skipped a beat. Detecting a heartbeat at this stage was critical to make sure the baby grows well; the radiologist had said. Sakhi's husband had displayed the same indifference he always did towards everything about his wife. He had stayed outside the room and when Sakhi had sent the nurse to let him know that all was not well, he had not bothered coming to her. Sakhi had stood up slowly. Her feet feeling like logs; all the energy drained out of them upon hearing the radiologist's verdict that this baby will need to be aborted. She had dragged herself to her gynaecologist's cabin with the reports from the imaging.

Having witnessed many such first pregnancies result in medical terminations due to various complications, the seasoned gynaecologist's face had held a knowing and comforting smile. She had convinced Sakhi that the reports indicated it would be unadvisable to continue with the pregnancy and that she would write her a medicine that would immediately terminate it. Sakhi's dreams, her desires to make this world a happy and fulfilling place for her child, her aspirations for her education, her child's future, everything had come crashing down in those thirty minutes but her husband was nowhere near her. She knew he would be unaffected by the loss and would be calmly reading a newspaper in the waiting area outside. She had walked outside, bought the prescribed medication, and gone home with her husband without a word being exchanged between them on the ride home. It was as if she had been riding next to a ghost. Her thoughts came back to the present as hunger gnawed at her insides. 'Where was that ghost now? How had he not come booming into her room asking where his lunch was?' Lost in her thoughts she walked towards his room to look in and spotted the huge picture frame. Her husband's eyes stared back at her from his photo that she herself had displayed near his work table after his death last year. That is when she was reminded of the reason for his absence. A fleeting thought peeped momentarily into her head. 'Was this why she was mindlessly making the garland until noon? Did she intend to adorn her dead husband's photo with flowers that were so much like her? Did she want to be with him despite him never wanting to be with her?'

She clenched her fists while these thoughts raced through her head and a single drop of blood oozed out of the wound where the needle had pricked her earlier. The sight of blood pulled Sakhi back to the day she took the medicine to terminate her pregnancy. She had experienced strong contractions and she had bled through the night. There was no one around to support or comfort her as she had wailed and doubled over in pain. She never knew when the pain had become so excruciating that she had succumbed to sleep. She had woken up the next morning, gathered the soiled sheets around her, and set about washing them amongst her many other daily chores. Something had snapped that day. Something that could never be mended. She knew things would never be the same with her husband.

As her memory increasingly failed her now, this was one day that she desperately wished would get wiped out of her recollections. That was not meant to be. She was slowly forgetting her address, her phone number, use of the television remote and many other routine things. These daily pieces of information would only slightly flash into her head and vanish almost as quickly as they had surfaced. Her kind neighbors would lead her home, as she would stand looking meek and lost, opposite her home, not knowing which way to head. But every single time there was a vacuous hole in her network of thoughts, with only a rapidly disappearing memory thread to hopelessly cling on to, the recollection of that fateful day, when she had to abort her child, would make its way through and spread its dark cloak over everything. 'Was it ever possible for her to forget the day she had lost the one person who could possibly have loved her back and cherished her presence?'. She rested herself on her husband's work table trying to calm her agitated thoughts. As her palms touched the table, she realized how dusty the room had become from neglect. But Sakhi could not bring herself to remember where she had kept the dusting cloth. She was not sure if her maid was coming over today so she could tell her to clean the room, if she remembered this chore by the time her maid arrived. 'Did she have a maid?' she wondered.

Sakhi had ignored her thirst for so long now that she started feeling dizzy. A sudden tightness grabbed at her heart. She felt a shooting pain in her left arm. She gasped for breath but did not have enough strength to take in air. She pressed her shoulder hard as the pain radiated all across her left side. Her knees buckled and she crashed on to the floor. As she fell, she spotted the garland of those bright orange and yellow flowers that sat on her sofa. They were called firecracker flowers – so called because the dried seeds of the plant disperse with an explosion when water hits them, typically during monsoon. Sakhi knew the garlands would stay fresh for at least a couple of days after *she* was gone. She asked herself, *'Would anybody notice she was no longer there? Or would her memory be erased from people's minds, as easily as most of her own were?'*